To my daughters:
Your spirit and compassion
make the world a better place.

ISBN: 9780578302836

Soldier Soup

Written by
Sharon Esposito

Illustrated by
Gabrielle Esposito

Chandler felt the cool breeze drift across her bare legs. She pulled her knees towards her, burying her feet in the warm blanket.

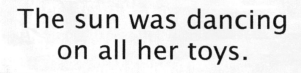

The sun was dancing
on all her toys.

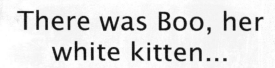

There was Boo, her
white kitten...

...her stuffed
animals on the
toy box...

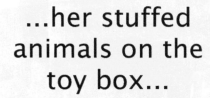

...and Baby was on the floor
eating a hot dog and donuts.

She sat up to see if Gabrielle was awake. There was a blanket fort stretched between their beds where they had been making magic potion cookies last night. Gabrielle's eyes were still closed.

Maybe Mom is awake." Chandler hopped out of bed and scurried to Mom's room.

Mom's bed always seemed like a mountain. It was much harder to climb on than her own.

"Mommy, wake up.
It's time to get up!"

Mom opened her eyes and smiled.
"Mommy, wake up.
It's time to get up!"

Mom laughed and said,
"Okay, okay, let's get up."

They went to the kitchen, and Chandler waited for Mom to bring the cereal. Then they hummed and danced as Mom made coffee and Chandler munched on her cereal.

Gabrielle came into the kitchen.
She mumbled "Good morning"
and poured her own cereal.

Gabrielle could do many things by herself.

Gabrielle was going to school now, and Chandler wanted to go too. Every day Chandler watched the kids at school skipping, laughing, and talking.
School must be lots of fun.
But every day Mom said it wasn't her turn yet.

Chandler understood taking turns, but it seemed like Gabrielle had plenty of turns already.

'I get to go to school today!'
Chandler shouted.

'Hooray!'

he ran to her closet...

...put on her shoes...

...and grabbed the new book bag she wasn't allowed to touch in what felt like forever.

"I'm ready for school!"

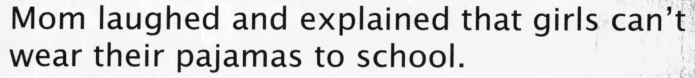

Mom laughed and explained that girls can't
wear their pajamas to school.
Finally she was dressed in her new yellow
pants and white shirt with a big yellow daisy

She grabbed her pink and white book bag.
Schools did not allow you in without this special
zippered bag. Sometimes they even put candy in
t, from what Gabrielle told her. Chandler couldn't
wait to get to school. What a fun place.

They said good-bye to Gabrielle. "I'll see you later! Have fun!"

"I will! Chandler, you're going to love school!"

Come on, come on!"
Today was *her* day for school!
Finally they made it to the classroom
where a nice lady welcomed them in…

"Wait!"
screamed Chandler.

She grabbed Mom
around the legs.
"I go with you, Mommy!"

"No, honey, Mommy
doesn't stay at school.
I'll be back to pick you
up later."

No, I go with you!" Chandler held tight to Mom and wondered why she was being left behind. She began to cry.

Mom kept saying it was okay, but it wasn't.

Who's going to help me put puzzles together?

Who's going to turn on the light in the bathroom?

Where will I sleep?

Who's going to hug me?

No, no, no, this is not okay.

"School is fun, Chandler! Look at all the toys here.
See the dress-up clothes?
See the stove and sink?"

Chandler stopped crying and looked at all the wonderful toys around her.
The lady walked up and took Chandler's hand. "Let me show you the stove, Chandler. My name is Mary."

Together they made soup, throwing lettuce – letters of the alphabet – even a toy soldier – into the pot.

"Mmm, that smells delicious!"

Chandler grinned proudly and continued cooking.

Mary had to hurry away when a little red-haired girl started screaming at the bird.

"Look at my soup, Mom!" Chandler
said with a proud smile.

There was no response.

Chandler looked around the room.
"Mom?"

Boys, girls...

...toys...

...bird...

...lady...

...but no Mom.

Chandler began to tremble. Where was Mom?
Did she leave me here? Would she ever come back?

Mary knelt in front of Chandler.
"Mommy will be back soon, Chandler."

"Soon?"

Chandler looked around at the other boys and girls. They were laughing and playing. No one was crying.

Mary led her and the other kids to a big circle in the middle of the room.

She read them stories, the they sang "Twinkle Twinkl Little Star" together

Chandler sang as loud as she could. Everyone would know that she knew this song. They swayed, marched, hopped, and jumped to lots of songs.

Just then a boy shouted "Mom!" and Chandler's eyes darted to the door. The boy ran to his mom and she picked him up.

"Mom?" Chandler said, but no one heard her and Mom wasn't there.

One by one other moms arrived, sweeping up the girls and boys, taking them away.

Chandler stared at the door, stretching her neck to find Mom, but she wasn't there.

Chandler wondered where Daddy was. Maybe he could save her.

Daddy wouldn't want her to stay here at night time. He needed her to help him take off the heavy boots he wore to work.

Yes, Daddy would save her.

Chandler walked up to Mary and asked, "Daddy coming?"

Chandler raised her head to see Mom standing there smiling with her arms spread wide...

...waiting for a hug
that was saved just
for Chandler.

Chandler ran
to her.

"Mommy!
You're back!
I missed you so
much!"

They grabbed Chandler's coat and headed out of the classroom, Chandler holding tight to Mom's hand.

She turned back to look at Mary who was standing in the doorway.

"Bye, see you next time!" she said with a wave.

Chandler looked up at Mom. "I had so much fun at school!"

"I'm so glad! See all the fun things you can do now that you're three?"

CPSIA information can be obtained
at www.ICGtesting.com
Printed in the USA
BVHW021459111121
621363BV00005B/210